MAMA SAYS

*A Book of Love for
Mothers and
Sons*

MAMA SAYS

A Book of Love for Mothers and Sons

by ROB D. WALKER

illustrations by

LEO & DIANE DILLON

THE BLUE SKY PRESS

An Imprint of Scholastic Inc.

New York

THE BLUE SKY PRESS

Text copyright © 2009 by Rob D. Walker

Illustrations copyright © 2009 by Leo & Diane Dillon

For information regarding permission, please write to: Permissions Department,

Scholastic Inc., 557 Broadway, New York, New York 10012.

SCHOLASTIC, THE BLUE SKY PRESS, and associated logos

are trademarks and/or registered trademarks of Scholastic Inc.

Library of Congress catalog card number: 2007029827

ISBN-13: 978-0-439-93208-0 / ISBN-10: 0-439-93208-4

10 9 8 7 6 5 4 3 2 1   09 10 11 12 13

Printed in Singapore   46

First printing, April 2009

Designed by Leo & Diane Dillon

and Kathleen Westray

For all the mothers everywhere who sacrifice *everything*—
time, money, and their entire youth—to raise
their children. Without you, there is no me.
God bless you all!
—R. D. W.

To Bonnie, Kathy, and Grace
The love is in the details. . . . Thank you.

And to the loving mothers of the world
—L. & D. D.

Mama says	ᎥᎥ ᎠᏗᏎ
Be good	ᏆᏍᏆ ᏈᏌᎶᏗ
Mama says	ᎥᎥ ᎠᏗᏎ
Be kind	ᏣᏢᏗ ᏈᏛᎶᏗ
Mama says	ᎥᎥ ᎠᏗᏎ
The rain will come	ᏆᏏ ᏣᎲ
But still the sun will shine	ᎠᏎᏃ ᏆᎥ ᎠᏍᏈᎶᏍᎶᏗ

Mama says	Мама говорит:
Be loving	Люби других.
Mama says	Мама говорит:
Be caring	Заботься о них.
Mama says	Мама говорит:
You've done God's will	Делись с ними.
Every time you're sharing	Бог велит быть
	Таким с другими.

Mama says	እማማ ትላለች
Be strong	ጠንካራ ሁን
Mama says	እማማ ትላለች
Be bright	ብሩህ ሁን
Mama says	እማማ ትላለች
Sometimes hard work	አንዳንድ ጊዜ ጠንካራ ሥራ
May keep you up at night	ሌሊት ሊያነቃህ ይችላል

Mama says	おかあさんはいう
Be honest	しょうじきに
Mama says	おかあさんはいう
Be true	せいじつに
Mama says	おかあさんはいう
To put my heart	こころをこめて
In everything I do	すべてのことに

Mama says	माँ कहती हैं,
Sometimes we cry	"कभी कभी हमें रोना आता है।"
Mama says	माँ कहती हैं,
Release	"शान्त हो जाओ।"
Mama says	माँ कहती हैं कि
That happiness	खुशी अन्दर से मिलती है।
Comes from inner peace	

Mama says	⊲ȧɑˡL ⊃ˤᏰ⊃∩ᒥᒪᒪˡL̇ˤᏰ
Be helpful	∆Ꮟ⊲ᏟᒪσˤᏰᒐᒻ⊲ˤᏰᒥᏟᒐᒧ
Mama says	⊲ȧɑˡL ⊃ˤᏰ⊃∩ˤᏰᒥᏟᒐᒪᒪˡL̇ˤᏰ
Be sure	⊃Ꮲᒻᒪᒻᒻ⊲ᒧ∩ᒧ
Mama says	⊲ȧɑˡL ⊲ᏒˤᏢᒧ⊃ˤᏰᒥᏟᒐᒪᒪˡL̇ˤᏰ
Success is when	∧ᒥˤᏰᒧˤᏢˤᏰᒥᏟᒧˤᒪᒧ∩ᒧ
You know you must endure	ᒥ∧ˤᏟ∆ᒧᒧˤᏰᒥᏟᒧ⊲ᏢᏜᒧ
	⊲ˤᒻᏢˤɑᒧˤᏰᒥᒧ⊲ˤ⊲ᒧ

Mama says	אִמָּא אוֹמֶרֶת
Have faith	תִּהְיֶה בַּטוּחַ
Mama says	אִמָּא אוֹמֶרֶת
Believe	תַּאֲמִין
Mama says	אִמָּא אוֹמֶרֶת
To trust in God	לִסְמוֹךְ עַל יְיָ
And let God take the lead	וְתֵן לַיְיָ לְהַנְחוֹת

Mama says
To be on time
Mama says
Be neat
Mama says
To walk with pride
And never drag my feet

Mama says	엄마가 말씀하셨어요.
Have courage	아무리 무서워도
Although I may be scared	씩씩하라구요.
Mama says	엄마가 말씀하셨어요.
To walk with care	조심조심 한걸음씩 나아가면
And I will be prepared	문제 없을 거라구요.

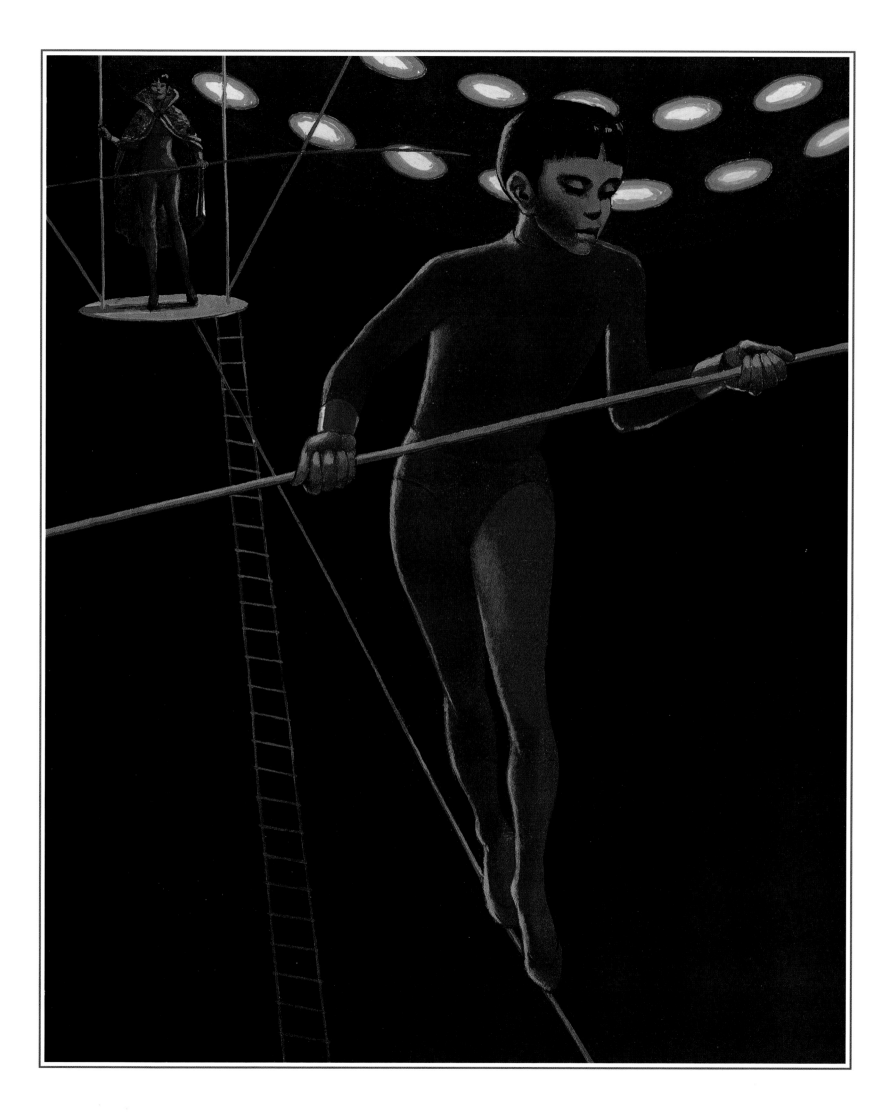

Mama says	ماما تقول
Embrace the moon	احتضن القمر
And marvel at the sun	وتأمّل الشمس بدهشة
Mama says	ماما تقول
To study stars	تفحّص النجوم
And make a wish on one	واطلب أمنية من إحداها

Mama says	Mama nin
Respect all life	Sapa sach'ata munarikuna
And treasure every tree	Tukuy ima kawsaqta much'ana
Mama says	Mama nin
Our planet needs	T'ikapuni, p'isqupuni, lachiwanapuni
Each flower, bird, and bee	Qhallallachin kay pachanchistaqa

Mama says	Mor siger
Help others	Hjælp andre
And be the best you can	Og gør dit bedste

I listened to what Mama said

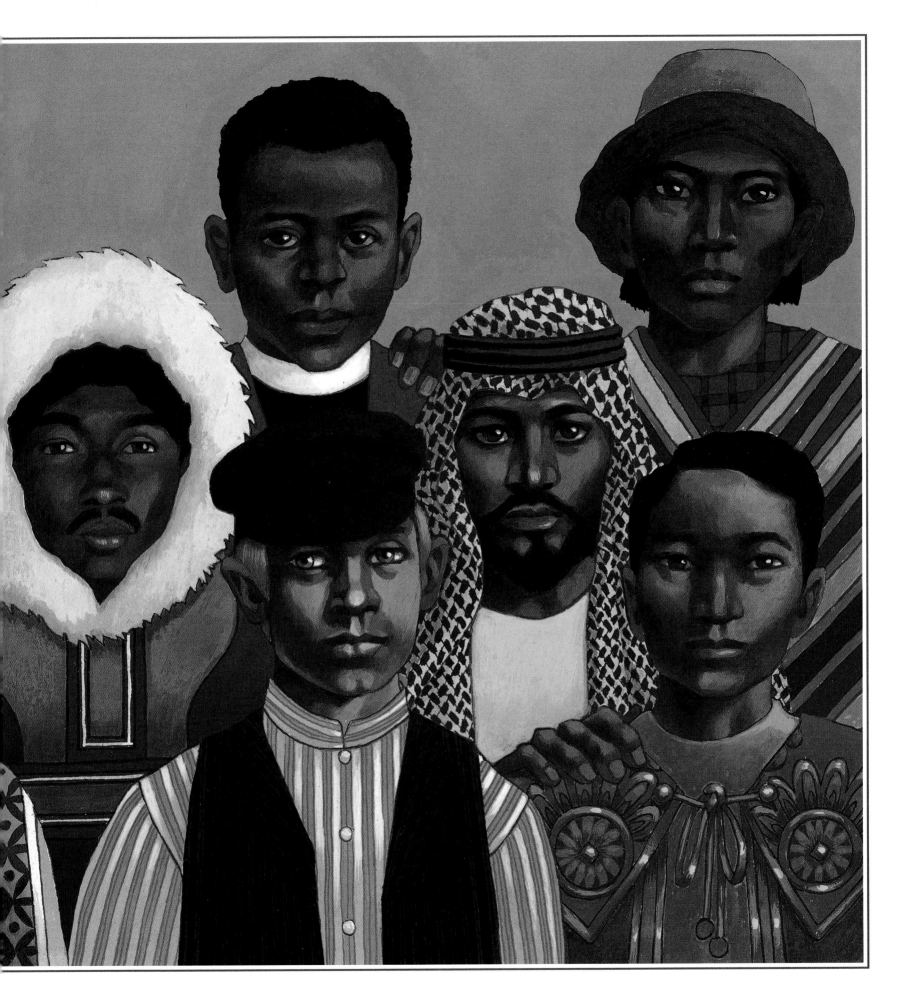

And now I am a man.

AFTERWORD

THROUGHOUT THE WORLD, people of all nations, cultures, and religions pass along their words of wisdom from generation to generation. At our best, we hope to help our children to have courage, be strong, show compassion, and be loving human beings. But our words are not enough. In this book, readers are invited into the private lives of a broad variety of families. Not only do loving parents provide guidance to their children in words—they also show the truth of their lessons through their actions and behavior. Helping those in need, standing up for what we believe in, and taking time to revel in the wonder of the natural world around us are only a few things that enrich our lives on a daily basis. In this respect—our ability to both give love and receive love—we are all alike. As the fabric of our world brings us closer together, let us celebrate our diversity and our common need for compassion, patience, faith, and a willingness to always look for the best in ourselves and others.

SPECIAL THANKS

Because languages are migratory, and so many variations and written interpretations are possible, we especially appreciate the efforts and contributions of the many language experts who helped us with the complicated and often very difficult translations in this book, including the following people:

Bo Taylor, Museum of the Cherokee Indian (Cherokee, page 6)
Irina Dolgova, Yale University (Russian, page 8)
Telahun Gebrehiwot, Harvard University (Amharic, page 10)
Mari Stever, Yale University (Japanese, page 12)
Mekhala Devi Natavar, Princeton University (Hindi, page 14)
Georges Filotas, Avataq Cultural Institute (Inuktitut, page 16)

Cantor David Berger (Hebrew, page 18)
Angela Lee-Smith, Yale University (Korean, page 22)
Nancy Coffin, Princeton University (Arabic, page 24)
Luis Morató-Lara, Penn State University (Quechua, page 26)
Rikke V. Landi, Danish American Society (Danish, page 28)
Dick, Dawn, and Bradley Weyiouanna

 CHEROKEE is the language of the Cherokee Native American people of North America. Cherokee is a southern Iroquoian language, and it is still spoken today.

 RUSSIAN is the official language of Russia and is one of the most widely used languages of Eurasia. It is spoken as a second language in most of the countries formerly of the Soviet Union.

 AMHARIC is spoken throughout present-day Ethiopia. It is a Semitic language, sharing its roots with Arabic and Hebrew. Amharic is also spoken in Egypt, Eritrea, Israel, and elsewhere.

 JAPANESE is predominantly spoken in Japan by more than 120 million people and also around the globe. Because of Japan's diverse geography, numerous versions of Japanese are spoken.

 HINDI is an official language of India and is spoken popularly throughout northern and central India. It is also spoken in Bangladesh, Mauritius, South Africa, Uganda, and Yemen.

 INUKTITUT is an Inuit language, spoken mainly in northern Canada. The Inuit languages and dialects are spoken across Alaska, through northern Canada, and on to Greenland and Russia.

 HEBREW is the native language of millions of people in Israel, where it is the official language, and the countless Jewish and Israeli communities around the world.

 ENGLISH is an official language of numerous countries, including the United States, Australia, Canada, India, Ireland, New Zealand, the Philippines, and the United Kingdom.

 KOREAN is the official language of North and South Korea. It is also spoken by millions of people in China, Japan, Kazakhstan, the United States, and Uzbekistan.

 ARABIC is widely spoken across, and frequently the premier language of, many Middle Eastern and northern African countries. Millions of people worldwide speak and read Arabic every day.

QUECHUA is an indigenous language of the Andean region of South America. Millions of people speak it in Argentina, Ecuador, Bolivia, Peru, northern Chile, and southern Colombia.

 DANISH is the official language of Denmark but is also spoken in northern Germany and the Faeroe Islands. Danish is spoken wherever its immigrants settle, as are all these languages.